VULGAR THE VIKING AND THE TERRIBLE TALENT SHOW

LOOK OUT FOR MORE STORIES OF MAYHEM AND CHAOS IN

VULGAR THE VIKING AND THE TERRIBLE TALENT SHOW

ODIN REDBEARD

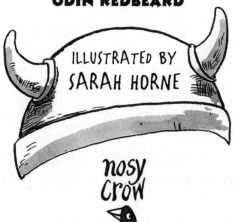

ILLUSTRATED BY
SARAH HORNE

nosy
crow

With special thanks to
Barry Hutchison

First published in the UK in 2013 by Nosy Crow Ltd
The Crow's Nest, 10a Lant St
London, SE1 1QR, UK

Nosy Crow and associated logos are trademarks and/or
registered trademarks of Nosy Crow Ltd

Text copyright © Hothouse Fiction, 2013
Illustrations © Sarah Horne, 2013

The right of Hothouse Fiction and Sarah Horne to be identified as the author
and illustrator respectively of this work has been asserted by them in accordance
with the Copyright, Designs and Patents Act 1988.

A CIP catalogue record for this book will be available from the British Library

Printed and bound in the UK by Clays Ltd, St Ives Plc

Papers used by Nosy Crow are made from wood grown in sustainable forests.

ISBN: 978 0 85763 062 9

www.nosycrow.com

CHAPTER ONE

SNOW DAY

Little flakes of white drifted in through the open windows of Vulgar's house. He shivered, half with cold and half with excitement. There was snow outside – snow! – but he was stuck inside with his parents.

"Can I go out to play?" he asked hopefully. He flattened down his wild, greasy hair and opened his eyes as wide

as he could. "Please?"

Vulgar's mum, Helga, looked up from her knitting. Helga was a big woman with enormous hands and the whalebone knitting needles looked tiny in her grasp. "No," she said. "It's too cold."

"Aw, Mum! But real Vikings don't mind the cold," Vulgar said. "We love it!"

"Not now," Helga sighed.

"Maybe later."

Vulgar slowly counted to three in his head. One. Two. Three.

"OK. How about now?"

Helga glanced over at her husband. "Harald. Tell him."

"Vulgar, listen to your mother," Harald said, without looking up.

Harald was not as big as his wife. Nowhere near it, in fact. Helga could have carried her husband in one hand, and still had room for her knitting. He was technically a Viking, but not the sort that Vulgar wanted to be. His beard was too wispy and his helmet was too small for a start. To make matters worse,

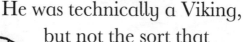

Harald never went looting or plundering. He didn't even own a longship! He cleaned toilets for a living and that, Vulgar thought, was the most un-Viking job anyone could ever do.

But then no one in the village of Blubber was very good at being a Viking. Vulgar was determined that one day he would show them all how it was supposed to be done!

Harald was sitting in the kitchen,

weaving a tapestry. Vulgar shook his
head in dismay – weaving, for goodness'
sake. It looked a bit like a gargoyle, or
some kind of horrible troll.

Vulgar tilted his head left and right,
trying to work out what the picture was.
"Is it a Frost Giant?" he asked. "You
know, one of the really ugly ones?"

"A Frost Giant?" said Harald.
He looked at
the tapestry.
"No, it's your
mother."

Vulgar stared
at the cloth,
then over at
his mum. "Oh
yeah," he
said, suddenly
seeing the
resemblance.

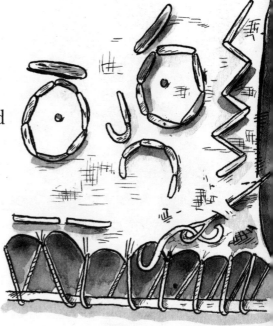

"So it is. That's amazing, Dad! You're so talented."

"Thank you," said Harald. "But you still can't go outside."

With a sigh, Vulgar stood up. Over in the corner his dog, Grunt, lay snoring. A big pot of stew bubbled on the fire.

Next to the fire sat a big pile of dried elk manure. Helga burned piles of the stuff during the winter to keep the house warm. It worked, but it also made the whole place stink of poo.

Vulgar gave the manure a poke. It had dried into a solid heap. It was almost the size of his head and perfectly round. He picked it up. Not too heavy, not too light. His mum and dad watched as he bounced the manure ball off his knee and began to play keepie-uppie.

"One, two, three…" he counted, juggling the hardened poo with his feet.

"Careful with that, Vulgar,"

Harald warned, then he ducked as the manure flew over his head and thudded against the wall.

"Sorry, I'm out of practice," Vulgar said as he scooped up his ball. He started again. "One, two, three, four, five…"

He lost control again and the dung bounced with a *boing* off Helga's cheek.

"Vulgar!" she snapped.

"Sorry, Mum, I didn't mean to hit you in the face with elk poo," Vulgar said.

"On the bright side, though, that was my new record!"

Helga picked a fleck of manure from her eyebrow and dropped it on to the floor. "I'm very happy for you," she said. "Now be careful."

"Will do!" Vulgar chirped. "Right, watch this. This is going to be the best yet."

He swung back his leg and kicked, but his aim was bad. Vulgar and his parents watched the manure go up, up, up into the air. They stared as it bounced off the ceiling, then they gasped as it landed with a soggy splat in the stew pot.

Helga gripped her knitting needles so tightly one of them snapped in half.

"OK," she muttered. "*Now* you can go outside."

Vulgar punched the air. "Yes!" He made a run for the door, but his mum got there before him.

"First," she said, "you have to wrap up warm."

Fifteen minutes later, Vulgar stood in the snow. A tiny patch of his face was visible. The rest of him was buried beneath a mountain of wool.

He wore a woolly jumper with a woolly cardigan on top. His sealskin shorts had been replaced by a pair of woolly trousers. A scarf was wrapped around his face, and his hands were trapped inside fluffy mittens. Vulgar was so bundled up that he could barely move.

On his head was a woolly hat. It was shaped like a Viking helmet, complete with knitted horns. It was, Vulgar thought, the itchiest, scratchiest hat in the world.

Grunt stood in the snow beside him, looking up.

"Don't you dare laugh," Vulgar warned, and Grunt gave a bark that sounded suspiciously like a snigger.

There was a crunch of footsteps through the snow. Vulgar looked up and saw his best friend, Knut, coming out to meet them. Knut looked like he always did – the same jumble of sackcloth clothing, the same helmet with one horn pointing the wrong way. He did have a scarf on, but it was wrapped around his waist like a belt.

"All right?" Knut said. "Seen my monster?"

Vulgar scratched his head. "What monster?"

"That one," said Knut, pointing to a huge snowman that stood over by his house. "It's a Snow Beast."

Vulgar peered up at the Snow Beast. It was almost as tall as his mum. He scratched his head and had an idea. "It needs something."

Knut frowned. "What?"

"A hat." Vulgar pulled off his itchy woollen hat and climbed on to Knut's back so he could reach the Snow Beast's head. "There," he said, giving his own head one final scratch. "Much better."

From somewhere nearby, they heard the sound of singing. Vulgar's eyes narrowed as he recognised the voice of Princess Freya. Putting his finger to his

lips, he led Knut and Grunt around a few stone huts until they spotted the princess. She was lying on the ground and waving her arms up and down, making angel shapes in the snow.

"What's she up to?" Knut whispered.

Vulgar shrugged. "No idea."

"Maybe she's fallen over and can't get up?"

"Maybe we should help her," Vulgar said. He and Knut both smirked. "Nah!"

They knelt down and squashed together some snowballs. Being careful to keep out of sight, Vulgar took aim, drew back his arm, and threw.

The snowball sailed through the air. Vulgar grinned. It was going to be a direct hit!

Then, just before the snowball struck her, Freya swiftly rolled out of the way. "Ha!" she cried. "I knew you'd turn up sooner or later."

The princess reached into the pockets of her furry waistcoat and pulled out two snowballs of her own. She hurled them both, and Vulgar and Knut gasped as the icy snow splattered across their faces.

"Right!" Vulgar cried,

grabbing for another snowball. "You asked for it!"

He was about to open fire when a low droning sound echoed around the village. It was the sound of the Official Announcement Horn.

Vulgar dropped his snowball as they all started trudging in the direction of the Great Hall. "Don't you go running off anywhere," he warned Freya. "After this, it's snowball time."

Freya cracked her knuckles. "Oh yes? Bring it on!"

CHAPTER TWO

THE BIG ANNOUNCEMENT

The horn blasted two more times in the next fifteen minutes. By the time it had sounded for a third time, everyone in Blubber was squashed into the Great Hall. They grumbled and complained, unhappy at having to leave their warm houses.

Still, the Official Announcement Horn meant only one thing – an official announcement – and everyone knew you didn't ignore an official announcement.

Vulgar, Knut and Freya stood right at the front of the crowd. With so many bodies crammed in, the hall was becoming very hot and Vulgar sweated inside his knitted outfit.

An old man with a bent back and crooked, wobbly legs hobbled out on to the stage. He waved a walking stick at the crowd and glared. "Right, you lot, that's enough," snapped Harrumf, the steward of the Great Hall. "Quit your whingein' an' open yer ears."

Harrumf rocked on his heels and

waited for the crowd to fall silent. When it eventually did, he knocked three times on the stage with his stick. *Thock. Thock. Thock.*

"Men, women an' little babes of Blubber," he began, "what a treat we 'ave in store for you on this fine winter's day."

"Oh, get on with it!" called someone from the crowd. Harrumf ignored him and carried on.

"You's a right lot of lucky so-an'-sos, you are. You ain't gonna believe who's waitin' in the wings to address you today."

"Is it King Olaf?" asked a woman near the front of the audience.

"It's always King Olaf," said a man at the back.

"Not always it ain't," said Harrumf. "It might not be 'im."

"Who is it, then?" shouted Vulgar.

Harrumf glanced at the curtain by the side of the stage. "Knnm Omnnn," he mumbled, too quietly for anyone to hear.

"What was that?"

"Speak up!"

Harrumf tutted. "King Olaf. You happy now?" He hobbled offstage again, muttering below his breath.

As the old man reached the curtain, a stomach emerged from behind it. The stomach was soon followed by the rest of King Olaf, who munched on some

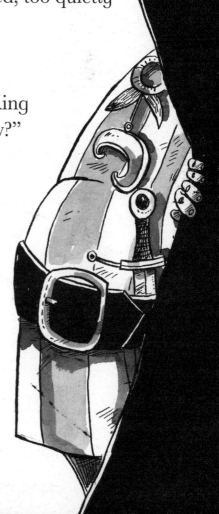

boar trotters as he shuffled across the
stage. A quiet ripple of applause went
around the room.

"Thank you, thank you," said Olaf,
spraying half-chewed boar trotters across
the front row. Vulgar picked a lump out

of his hair and secretly stuck it to Freya's
back. "I expect you're wondering why I
summoned you all here."

Vulgar raised a hand. "Are there
dragons?"

King Olaf frowned. "What?"

"Dragons," said Vulgar. "Is it because loads of dragons are swooping in to attack the village, and you need us to fight them off?"

"Um… no."

Vulgar lowered his hand. "Oh," he said. "Pity."

"Yes, well…"

"Giants, then?" asked Vulgar hopefully. "Did you want to tell us about an army of giants that want to grind our bones and—?"

"A talent contest," said the king, cutting Vulgar short.

Vulgar glanced at Knut. "A talent contest?"

"Yes." Olaf nodded. "To brighten up the long winter ahead, I thought we would have a talent contest."

"Right. So definitely not giants, then?"

The king shook his head crossly at
Vulgar, then turned to the rest of the
audience. "The contest shall be open to
all Blubberers. If you have a talent—"

"Ha! Fat chance," snorted Harrumf
from offstage.

"—then this is your chance to share it
with us all," said Olaf, ignoring the old
man. "It doesn't matter if you sing, dance
or do amusing things with pickled herring
– this Saturday will be your chance to
shine as the Great Hall hosts the first ever
Blubber Talent Contest!"

A much more enthusiastic round of
applause went around the room, and
the audience began to chatter with
excitement. A talent contest! They'd
never had a talent contest before. King
Olaf left the stage and the crowd began
to hurry out before Harrumf came back.

Down at the front, Vulgar turned to

Knut. "Odin's elbows! This is going to be brilliant!" he said, bouncing up and down with excitement.

"Are you going to enter?" Knut asked.

"Of course I'm going to enter!" Vulgar replied. "And I'm *definitely* going to win!"

"Great! What are you going to do?"

Vulgar thought about this. If he was going to win he had to do something amazing. Something spectacular. Something that would blow everyone's eyebrows off.

"Oh, I know, I know!" he cried, slipping his hand up inside his woolly jumper and trapping it beneath a sweaty armpit.

He pumped his arm furiously up and down and a series of loud squelchy trumping noises echoed around the hall. "I'm going to do that!"

Knut wasn't sure. "I like it," he said. "But I don't know if anyone else will."

"Are you crazy? They'll love it!" Vulgar pumped his arm again and several more soggy parps rang out. Knut shook his head.

"Can you do anything else?"

Vulgar thought some more. "I could… juggle elk manure."

Knut wrinkled his nose. "Not very exciting, though, is it?"

"I could set it on

fire first!"

Knut shook his head again. "Harrumf wouldn't let you in case you burned the place down," he said. "Or decorated the walls with elk poo."

"I could shove a whole rock cake in my mouth."

"You do that every day."

Vulgar sighed. This was proving harder than he thought. "Two rock cakes?"

Freya stepped between them, her hands on her hips. "Ha! You two wouldn't know talent if it smacked you on the helmet with a broadsword. There's only one way you have a chance of winning."

"Oh yeah?" asked Vulgar. "What's that?"

"I'm going to sing," the princess said, ignoring the question. "It's a beautiful love song about the goddess Freya, whom I was named after."

"Sounds horrible," Vulgar sniffed. "How does it help me win?"

Freya smiled sweetly. "Because it's a duet. I need someone to sing with me."

Vulgar's jaw dropped open. "What?"

"I'd be the goddess Freya, obviously. You'd be my true love, Od."

"I'd rather arm-wrestle a giant squid!" Vulgar spluttered.

Freya scowled. "Fine! But you'll never win without me! Blubber might have talent, but you don't!"

"Want a bet? I've got *loads* of talent," Vulgar insisted. "In fact, I've got an amazing top-secret act that's bound to win. It's much better than some stupid love song."

"Oh yes? What is it, then?" Freya demanded.

Vulgar crossed his arms. "Not telling," he said, turning away. "It's a secret."

The princess stomped her foot on the stone floor. "Fine!" she snapped, then she stormed off towards the exit.

"So what's the top-secret act, then?" Knut asked.

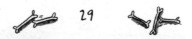

Vulgar shrugged. "No idea. I just said that to get rid of her." He sighed and looked around the now almost empty Great Hall. "There must be something I can do."

He stopped when he spotted the tapestries hanging on the wall. They showed great moments of Viking history, back when Vikings behaved the way Vikings should.

Vulgar stared at the largest tapestry. It showed the legendary Sven the Dragon-Slayer. In the picture, Sven was pinning a large green dragon to the ground while kicking it up the bottom. Underneath the scene was a title – Booting Some Dragon Bum. It had always been one of Vulgar's favourite stories, and he suddenly knew how he was going to win the talent show.

"I'm going to re-enact the legend of Sven the Dragon-Slayer," he cried. "With fighting and dragons and giants and treasure and all that stuff. I'm going to show everyone in Blubber how *real* Vikings are supposed to behave!"

Vulgar's eyes sparkled as he turned to Knut and flashed him a broad grin. "What could possibly go wrong?"

CHAPTER THREE

FULL MESS REHEARSAL

Next morning, Vulgar was up and dressed early. It was Friday, which meant there was only one day until the talent contest. He had to fit in lots of practice before then if he was going to win.

There was a knock at the door. Down on the floor, Grunt raised his head and let out a lazy woof. Vulgar opened the door and Knut shuffled in. Grunt closed his eyes and promptly went back to sleep.

"There you are!" Vulgar cried, shutting the door behind his friend.

Knut yawned and rubbed his eyes. "Here I am," he nodded. Then he added, "Why am I here?"

"To help me with the act!"

"Oh yeah," said Knut, yawning again. "I forgot." He looked around the hut. "Where are your mum and dad?"

"They're at the Great Hall. They've decided to enter the contest, too."

"What's their talent?" Knut asked.

"Dancing," said Vulgar.

"Dancing?" asked Knut.

Vulgar nodded. "Dancing," he said, and both boys shuddered at the thought. "Still, it means we can rehearse in peace."

"You mean *you* can rehearse in peace," Knut said.

Vulgar grinned. "Yes, well, I wanted to talk to you about that. In the story, Sven fights an evil dwarf, a wicked giant and a fearsome dragon, so he can rescue some silly princess and – more importantly – collect a huge treasure chest and a magical golden helmet."

Knut nodded. Everyone knew the story of Sven the Dragon-Slayer. "That's a lot of characters. How are you going to play them all?"

"I'm not," said Vulgar. "You are."

"What?!" spluttered Knut. "No way!"

"Come on, Knut," pleaded Vulgar. "I can't be Sven the Dragon-Slayer and the evil dwarf at the same time. I'd be fighting myself. Everyone would laugh, and the legend of Sven isn't supposed to be funny."

Knut blew out his cheeks. "I dunno, Vulgar. All those people looking at me…"

"But they won't be looking at you, they'll be looking at me. I'm the star. All eyes will be on me."

"Yeah, but…"

"Come on, it'll be great!" Vulgar said. "And if you don't help there's no chance

I can win."

Knut sighed. "OK, fine," he said. "But you'd better not make me look stupid."

Vulgar smiled innocently. "As if I would! Now, first things first. We need a name. Any ideas?"

"Vulgar and Knut?"

Vulgar tapped his chin. "Too obvious. How about we call ourselves… By Far the Greatest Viking Actors in All the World?"

"It's a bit long, innit?"

"Maybe," Vulgar admitted. "What's that other word for actors, again?"

"Posers?" suggested Knut. "Show-offs?"

"No, no. Bards, that's it. We can be the Bards of Blubber!" Vulgar clapped his hands. "Now, let's rehearse. You be the evil dwarf and I'll be Sven."

Knut nodded. "Right. What should I do?"

"Just, you know. Be evil. And small."

Knut considered this. Then he dropped to his knees and went, "Grrr."

"Brilliant!" cheered Vulgar. He picked up a sword he'd made from two pieces of wood. He waved it around in front of him. "Then I'll do this!"

With a loud battle-cry, Vulgar began swinging the sword. He twirled to the left. He spun to the right. He jumped up and down and swung the sword around in a wide circle. There was a smash as the sword knocked over the clay cooking pot.

"Now you're in trouble," Knut said, but Vulgar snatched up the pot's lid and examined it. "This'll make a brilliant shield," he said. "Now you'd better start practising to be a giant. Here."

Vulgar handed Knut two long pieces of wood with string attached. "I've made you some stilts."

Knut sat down and tied the stilts on to his boots. "Help me up," he said, holding out an arm. With a grunt, Vulgar heaved his friend up on to his feet. Knut teetered unsteadily.

"Can you balance?" Vulgar asked.

"Yeah, I'm fine," Knut said, and promptly fell over. As he fell, he grabbed for the kitchen table.

The kitchen table fell, too.

There was a loud crack of splintering wood and the table broke in two. Knut looked up at his friend. "Can I be a giant later?"

Vulgar shrugged. "OK. Now you can practise being the dragon."

"I don't want to be the dragon as well," Knut said. "It's hard enough being a dwarf *and* a giant."

"Well, who's going to be the dragon, then?"

Over by the fire, Grunt let out a loud snore. A grin spread across Vulgar's face.

"Aha! Grunt can be our dragon."

At the sound of his name, Grunt opened one eye, trumped loudly, then fell back to sleep. Vulgar hopped up and down with excitement. "This is going to be brilliant!" he exclaimed. "Ready for more rehearsing?"

Knut groaned, but before they could get back to practising, the door swung open. Vulgar's mum and dad danced in, twirling cheek-to-cheek. Because Harald was much shorter than his wife, Helga was carrying him. They froze when they saw the broken table and the smashed cooking pot.

"Hi, Mum, hi, Dad," said Vulgar cheerfully. "You're back early."

"Vulgar!" growled Helga. "What have you been doing?"

"Practising," Vulgar said.

"Practising for what? An earthquake?

Look at the mess."

Vulgar looked at the floor and blinked, as if only noticing the mess for the first time. "Oh," he said. "Yeah. Um… sorry."

"Tidy this up," said Helga.

"But, Mum!"

Helga released her grip on her husband. He gave a short scream as he dropped to the floor. "Tidy it up,

Vulgar," he repeated. "Now!"

Grumbling, Vulgar and Knut set to work cleaning the hut and fixing the kitchen table. "When I'm a famous actor I'll have people to tidy up after me," Vulgar moaned, as they swept and scrubbed and hammered.

At last, the kitchen looked tidy. The cooking pot was still broken, and the table wobbled a bit, but Vulgar and Knut had done their best.

"Right," said Helga when they were finished. "Now I've arranged something exciting for you. King Olaf has invited you round to play with Princess Freya."

Vulgar and Knut both gasped. "What? No way!"

"Oh, come on now," said Harald. "She's a lovely girl. You'll have a great time."

"I'd rather dress as a fish and go

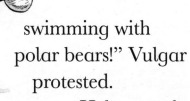

swimming with
polar bears!" Vulgar
protested.

Helga cracked
her knuckles
and glared at
Vulgar. "That could be arranged. Now
get going. It means you're out of my hair
for a few hours."

Without any effort, Helga picked both
boys up by the back of their shirts and
carried them to the door. They each let
out an *oof* as she dropped them on the
front step.

"But… but…" began Vulgar, still
trying to find an excuse not to go, "I'm
hungry. I haven't had lunch."

A bundle of stale rolls were shoved into
his arms. "There," said Helga, "now go!"

And before Vulgar could argue any
more, the door slammed shut in his face.

CHAPTER FOUR

THE BREAK-IN

Vulgar and Knut talked about the talent show as they slid their way along the icy path that led to the castle.

"What about the treasure?" Knut asked.

"What about it?"

"Well, do you have any?"

Vulgar thought about it. "No. We'll have to use pretend treasure."

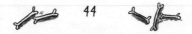

"It'll have to look like gold," Knut said. "Where could we find something like that?"

They slid on in silence for a few moments, then Vulgar looked down at the rolls in his arms. The bread was a sort of orangey-yellow colour and looked a bit like pale gold. "We could use these!"

"Aren't you going to eat them?"

"Are you crazy?" scoffed Vulgar. He knocked two rolls together. They made a sound like rock smashing against rock. "I'd break my teeth!"

Vulgar slipped the rolls into his pockets and the two friends continued on towards the castle. The closer they got, the slower they went. Neither one liked the idea of playing with Freya, but they also didn't like the idea of being made to swim with polar bears.

Lots of parents made silly threats to

their children, the difference was that Helga actually went through with them. Vulgar could still remember the time she'd tied him to a tree for refusing to go to bed when told. Seven hours he'd been there. It wouldn't have been so bad if she'd tied him the right way up.

At last they arrived at the castle's towering doors. There was a metal dragon mounted on them, resting on an iron hoop. Vulgar lifted the metal ring and thumped it against the door

a few times. From inside the castle they heard the sound of shuffling footsteps.

One of the doors opened a crack and a wrinkled face appeared in the gap. "Oh," sneered Harrumf. "It's you. You'll be wanting to see Princess Freya."

"Not really," said Vulgar, sighing. "But if we must."

Harrumf stood back and let the door swing open. Then the old man led them slowly through the castle corridors.

Vulgar had never been in the castle before, and nor had Knut. They walked along in a daze, admiring the armour that stood at every corner, and the weapons that hung from every wall.

After several minutes of walking, they arrived at a door with frilly lace hung around the edges, and a handle shaped like a love heart.

"I think I'm going to be sick," said Vulgar.

"Don't you dare," Harrumf warned. "It's me what'd have to clean it up."

The old man rapped his bony knuckles on the door. A voice inside called, "Come in," and then Harrumf shuffled off along the corridor, leaving the boys to it.

Cautiously, Vulgar pushed open the door. He let out a loud groan when he saw Princess Freya. She was sitting on the floor, surrounded by a circle of dolls. Some of the dolls wore baby clothes. Others wore gowns. Vulgar swallowed.

"Yep," he said. "I'm definitely going to be sick."

Freya looked up at Vulgar and Knut. "Well, come in, then," she snapped. "These babies won't feed themselves."

Vulgar and Knut exchanged a worried

glance. "Er…
what?"

"The babies," Freya repeated
firmly. She held up two leather baby
bottles. "They need feeding. Now."

The princess glared long and hard at
the boys until Knut couldn't stand it any
longer. He took one of the bottles, sat
down, and picked up the nearest doll.
Vulgar couldn't believe his eyes.

"What are you doing?! Have you gone
mad?"

Knut shrugged and rammed the end of
the bottle in the dolly's mouth.

"Now you," Freya said. She tossed the
bottle to Vulgar. "Feed the baby or I'm
telling my dad you were horrible to me."

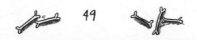

Vulgar snorted. "So?"

"And then he'll tell your mum," Freya added.

"Oh," said Vulgar, his face turning pale. He sat down and picked up a doll.

"Not that one!" Freya snapped. "That's not a baby."

Vulgar looked the doll up and down. "Isn't it?"

"It's wearing a ball gown. How many babies have you ever seen wearing a ball gown?"

Vulgar frowned. "What's a ball gown?"

"It doesn't matter," sighed Freya. She handed him the doll she had been holding. "That one needs burping."

Vulgar hesitated. "You do know they're not real babies, right?"

"I know that," Freya said. "It's called 'a game'."

"This is a game?" said Knut in amazement. "I thought it was some kind of punishment."

BURRRRRP!

Freya turned and glared at Vulgar. "Wow, the baby really did need to burp," he said, grinning. He let out another loud burp and the room was filled with the smell of last night's supper. "Better out than in."

Knut giggled. "I think mine has done a poo," he said. He shoved the doll's bottom towards Freya's nose. "Sniff that. Does that smell like poo to you?"

"Stop it!" Freya snapped. She snatched the dolls from the boys and set about positioning them back on the floor. "You've ruined the game now."

Vulgar leaned over to Knut and jabbed him with an elbow. "Here, we should borrow one of Freya's dresses," he said in a whisper.

"Why?"

"For the talent contest. For when you're playing the princess."

It took a few seconds for Knut's brain to figure out what Vulgar meant.

"I'm not wearing a dress!" he cried at last.

"You have to," Vulgar protested. "Who else is going to play the princess?"

Freya quietly cleared her throat. "Did someone say 'princess'?" she asked, smiling sweetly.

"Yes! She could do it!" Knut said. "Vulgar and me are doing a play about Sven the Dragon-Slayer for the talent show. I'm a dwarf and a giant."

"A dwarf and a giant?"

"Not at the same time, obviously. Vulgar's dog is going to be the dragon, but we need someone to be the princess."

Freya held her head high. "I'd make a terrific princess. I've had lots of practice."

"No," Vulgar said, crossing his arms. "No way."

"Sven the Dragon-Slayer, he found a magical golden helmet, didn't he?" said Freya slyly.

Vulgar narrowed his eyes suspiciously. "Yes. So?"

"So my dad has the only golden helmet in the whole country. You could borrow it."

"Could we?" Vulgar gasped.

"*If* you let me be the princess in the play." Freya smirked. "What do you say?"

The door to King Olaf's bedroom creaked as Freya eased it open. A loud snoring came from within. It was the sort of sound a bear might make if it were choking on a hedgehog. The king was having his Royal Nap.

"Where's the helmet?" Vulgar whispered. Freya pointed to the bed.

"There."

Vulgar looked. "Where?" he said, and then he saw it. "You have *got* to be kidding me."

Freya shrugged. "He likes to sleep with it on. He says it brings him good dreams."

"Well, it's turning into a nightmare for me," Vulgar muttered. "Let's come back when he's not here."

"No use," whispered Freya. "He keeps it locked up when he's not wearing it. It's now or never."

Vulgar rubbed his hands together. "Right then. I guess it's now."

Being careful not to make a sound, Vulgar and Freya tiptoed into the room. Knut stood outside, keeping guard. If they got caught, they'd be in deep trouble.

Slowly, Vulgar crept towards the bed.

Halfway there, King Olaf stopped snoring. Vulgar froze and held his breath.

"Hello, Mr Potato," the king mumbled. "What lovely shoes you have."

Vulgar blinked. He hadn't been expecting that. He looked back at Freya.

"He talks in his sleep," whispered the princess. "Now, hurry."

Vulgar continued on towards the head of the bed. He could see right up King Olaf's royal nostrils. The king's mouth was hanging open. A river of drool trickled into his beard.

At last, Vulgar was within grabbing distance of the helmet. His heart thumped so loudly he was sure it would wake the king, but Olaf was still grunting like a wild boar. With a final glance back at Freya, Vulgar took a deep breath then reached out for the golden helmet.

"Ducks?" spluttered King Olaf, suddenly sitting upright. "On a Tuesday?"

It took all Vulgar's willpower not to cry out in fright. He stuffed a hand into his mouth, stifling a loud gasp before it could escape. King Olaf was sitting up, but his eyes were still closed. He began to snore again. Vulgar quickly snatched the helmet off the king's head just before he lay down again.

The helmet was heavier than it looked and Vulgar very nearly dropped it. When he was sure he had it safely in his hands,

he turned and grinned at Freya. His grin
fell away when he heard Knut cough
loudly outside the door. That was the sign
for danger. Someone was coming!

Moving as quickly as they dared,
Vulgar and Freya darted out of the room.
They emerged to see Harrumf hobbling
towards them. "What you doing?"
Harrumf demanded.

Vulgar quickly
shoved the helmet
up inside his tunic,
but it made his
stomach look
huge. He
wrapped his
arms across
himself, trying
to hide the bump.
Harrumf glared
suspiciously at them.

"Hello, Harrumf," said Freya sweetly. "We were just saying hello to my dad."

Harrumf peeked in through the open door. King Olaf was still fast asleep on the bed.

"He, er, didn't say it back," Freya said, smiling innocently.

Harrumf peered at the lump beneath Vulgar's tunic. "What you got there?"

"A tummy bug," said Vulgar, thinking fast. He bent over and groaned as if in pain. "I really need to go to the toilet."

Harrumf prodded him with his cane. "Well, get a move on, then. I don't want to be cleanin' up your mess."

"Thanks," said Vulgar. He grabbed Knut by the arm and together they raced off down the corridor. Freya called after them as they ran.

"Hey, wait! We haven't even had a tea party yet!"

But the only reply was the clatter of the castle's front door as Vulgar and Knut ran out into the snow.

CHAPTER FIVE

THE SHOW BEGINS

"Hurry up, Vulgar," bellowed Helga.
"The show starts in fifteen minutes."

"Coming, Mum!" replied Vulgar in
a muffled voice.

He was sitting on the end of his bed,
fixing a fake beard to his face with glue.
He had made the beard from orange
wool he'd found in Helga's knitting
basket, and the glue he'd mixed himself

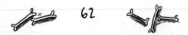

from snot and pond slime.

"How do I look, Grunt?" he asked, but Grunt was too busy chewing on his fake wings to reply. "Don't eat your costume," Vulgar told him. "Bad dog."

Snatching up his homemade sword and shield, Vulgar led Grunt into the kitchen. He stopped when he saw his parents.

"What… are… you… wearing?"

"Ta-daa!" said Harald. "What do you think?"

He and Helga both gave a twirl, showing off the outfits they had made. Harald wore a long coat covered with hundreds of sparkly little stones. Bits of whalebone had been shaped into a big letter "H" and stuck to his back.

Helga's outfit was nothing like her husband's outfit. It was nothing like anything Vulgar had ever seen her wearing before, either. It was a black dress with only one shoulder strap. Her bare biceps bulged whenever she moved her arms. The dress was so short Vulgar could see his mum's hairy knees. He'd never seen his mum's knees before. He hoped he'd never see them again.

Helga also had a letter
"H" on her back. It was the only
bit of the costume that didn't make
Vulgar shudder.

"I think I've sprained my eyes," he
squeaked, then they all left the house and
hurried over to the Great Hall.

Torches burned all around the hall,
making it look spectacular in the evening
gloom. Harald and Helga joined the
back of the queue at the front door, but
Vulgar didn't want to wait.

"See you inside!" he chirped, then he
and Grunt ducked and weaved past the
rest of the queue and squeezed into the
hall itself. Once inside, Vulgar spotted
Knut sitting near the front. There was an
empty seat beside him.

It wasn't until Vulgar was in the seat that he realised Freya was sitting on the other side of him. "You were almost late," she said.

Vulgar shrugged. "Almost late is the same as being on time."

Freya tutted.

Vulgar turned his back on her and spoke to Knut. "Did you bring the props?"

Knut frowned. "The props?"

"The golden helmet," Vulgar whispered. "The treasure?"

"I thought you were bringing them."

"No!" Vulgar cried. "You were bringing them! I gave them to you, remember?"

Knut grinned and held up a bag. "Just kidding. Got them here."

Vulgar gave a sigh of relief, then looked back over his shoulder. The hall was almost full now. Harald and Helga waved as they took their seats a few rows back. They were both carrying bags of rock cakes they'd bought on the way in.

A hush fell over the audience as the candles around the hall were snuffed out, leaving only the stage lit up. "Ladies an' gentle-thingies," said a voice from offstage. Everyone recognised it as Harrumf. "It's Saturday night. It's the Great Hall. It's Time. To Face. His Highness!"

King Olaf waddled on to the stage. He waved to the crowd, then took a seat at the long wooden judge's table that had been placed in front of the stage.

"An' joinin' his most royal of

royalnesses on the judging panel tonight is the one, the only… Harrumf Sockson!"

Harrumf stepped on to the stage and was met by stony silence. The old man tutted as he hobbled down the steps and over to the table. "Charming," he muttered, then he took his seat beside King Olaf.

"Our first contestant is a local lad," Harrumf announced. "He's gonna tell us some jokes an' that. Put your 'ands together for Magnus the Magnificent!"

The audience clapped politely as a short, stocky Viking shuffled nervously on to the stage. He blinked in the glow of the candles and wiped a smear of sweat from his forehead.

"It's me, Magnus the Magnificent, and I'm here to tickle your funny bone!" he announced in a shaky voice. He smiled down at the audience. Nobody smiled back. "Here's one for you," he said. "What do you get… no, not 'What do you get', that's wrong. Where do Viking babies sleep?"

"In a bed," shouted a voice from the crowd.

"N-no. In a norsery!" laughed Magnus. He stared expectantly at the audience. "Get it? Another name for a Viking is a Norseman. Norse. Nursery."

At the back of the hall, someone coughed.

"You don't get it, do you?" said Magnus.

"We should 'ave some sort of buzzer," said Harrumf loudly. "So we can buzz 'em off when they're rubbish."

Magnus looked hurt. "I'm not rubbish!"

"Come on," Harrumf snorted. "I've had funnier war wounds. Get off the stage."

"They don't want me to leave," Magnus insisted. He looked out to the audience. "You don't want me to leave, do you?"

A single rock cake came spinning through the darkness. It bounced off

Magnus's forehead with a hollow clonk. Several more of the rock-hard buns came flying at him as the

audience began to boo.

"Get off!"

"You're terrible!"

At the front of the audience, Vulgar watched as Magnus shielded his head with his arms and ran off the stage. "Wow, he was awful."

The next act was introduced. It was Torsten the Tangled, who claimed he could escape from any trap. The crowd held its breath as he waddled onstage wrapped in thick iron chains.

"My fellow Blubberers," he said, "before your very eyes, I, Torsten the Tangled, will free myself from these chains in less than ten seconds. If you'd like to begin the countdown… now!"

Torsten began wriggling furiously as the audience started to count backwards. "Ten. Nine. Eight." There was a moment of confused muttering.

Freya shook her head. "Seven!" she said loudly.

"Seven," chimed the crowd. "Six. Five. Four."

Torsten bent double and twisted his arms.

"Three. Two."

Torsten straightened up and twitched his head.

"One!"

Torsten fell face-first on to the floor and lay motionless. The chains were still wrapped tightly around him.

"Um," he said at last. "Could someone call the blacksmith? I appear to be stuck."

As a rain of rock cakes fell on him,

Torsten rolled off the stage.

"Good effort," said King Olaf politely. "Better luck next time."

"With any luck they'll never let 'im out," Harrumf mumbled.

Vulgar gave Knut a nudge. "This is going to be easy. We're *bound* to win. The other acts are terrible!"

Next up was Sigrid the Shrill. She was a large woman – almost as large as Helga – who believed she could sing. She was wrong. The noise she made when she opened her mouth was like nothing Vulgar had ever heard. He clamped his hands over his ears and was relieved when a rock cake thonked her on the head and sent her running for cover.

"Blimey, I 'aven't heard a noise like that since King Olaf shut his fingers in 'is bedroom door," Harrumf said. The king shot him a dirty look, and Harrumf quickly looked down at his notes.

"An' now," announced Harrumf. "The Dancin' H's. Who's that, then?"

Harald and Helga jumped to their feet, smiling broadly. They waved to Vulgar as they passed. A man stood at the back of the stage holding a set of wooden pipes. As Helga and Harald took their positions, the man began to play.

Vulgar sank lower into his seat as he watched his mum and dad spin and twirl on the stage. Helga carried Harald in

her arms and occasionally tossed him
up into the air. She hoisted him over one
shoulder then flipped him on to her back.
He swung down beneath her legs before
being lifted like a javelin above her head.

The crowd went "Oooh!" as Helga
balanced Harald on one hand, then rose
to their feet and clapped as she bent her
husband backwards and kissed him on
the lips.

When the applause had died down, Harald and Helga turned to the judges to await their verdict.

"That was like watching a polar bear wrestle a baby seal," Harrumf said. He wiped a tear from the corner of one eye. "It was the most beautiful thing what I ever saw."

"Bravo," agreed King Olaf. Even Vulgar had to admit they were pretty good.

"What's next, Harrumf?" the king asked. Harrumf peered at his notes.

"Oh yeah," he said with a scowl. "It's the legend of Sven the Dragon-Slayer."

"Here we go," whispered Vulgar, and with that the Bards of Blubber took to the stage.

CHAPTER SIX

LAUGHTER DISASTER

Vulgar stood on the stage and peered at the sea of faces watching him. Butterflies fluttered in his belly and he suddenly forgot why he was even there.

"Ready?" whispered Freya. Vulgar stared at her.

"Ready for what?" he whispered back.

Freya rolled her eyes. "To start the show."

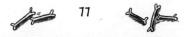

"Oh yeah, the show," Vulgar said out loud, and there was a chuckle from the audience. He patted down his false beard. "Right. Here goes."

Raising his wooden sword, Vulgar began to hack and slash across the stage, fighting his way through an army of imaginary Vikings.

"Have that," he called. "And some of that. And one of these!"

Sitting on the front of the stage, Freya began to narrate the story. "Sven sets off to find the legendary golden helmet of Valhalla. He battles…" Freya glanced at

Vulgar, who was still twirling and swiping with the sword. "…Um, something, until he meets an evil dwarf."

Vulgar stopped slashing with the sword. He looked expectantly at the curtain at the side of the stage, but no one appeared.

"I said, he meets an evil dwarf," Freya shouted.

"Oh, that's me," muttered a voice from offstage. The audience giggled as Knut shuffled out on his knees.

At once, Vulgar leapt into action. He 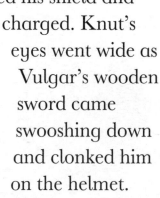 raised his shield and charged. Knut's eyes went wide as Vulgar's wooden sword came swooshing down and clonked him on the helmet.

"Ow! What did you do that for?" Knut demanded. The audience chortled.

"Because you're an evil dwarf."

Knut pushed his helmet back and rubbed his head. "You don't know I'm evil. You just met me. We could've been friends!"

Vulgar lowered his sword. "Oh. Um. Sorry."

The crowd laughed louder than ever.

"Too late now," muttered Knut. "You've blown it." And he turned and waddled offstage on his knees.

"After defeating the evil dwarf," continued

Freya, "Sven was confronted by an enormous giant."

"Give us a minute," called Knut from the wings. There was a clattering as he stood up on the homemade stilts. "Right," he announced, "I'm ready no-owwwww!"

Knut ran on to the stage, struggling to keep his balance. "Look out!" he cried as he wobbled towards the edge. Vulgar couldn't bring himself to look. He covered his eyes just as Knut toppled off the stage and landed in the audience.

Vulgar opened his eyes to see Knut upside down in Sigrid the Shrill's lap. "There, giant," he said, pointing the

sword at Knut as he slid down on to the
floor. "Let that be a lesson to you!"

The hall was filled with the sound of
laughter. Vulgar blushed. This wasn't
going well at all. The story of Sven
the Dragon-Slayer was supposed to be
thrilling and scary, not funny.

Freya continued the story. "Once the
giant was defeated, Sven found the
treasure he had been seeking."

Knut kicked off his stilts and scrambled
back up on to the stage. He disappeared
behind the curtain. A moment later,
a small wooden chest slid out from
underneath it.

"Treasure. Great!" Vulgar cried.

"But the treasure was guarded by a
fierce dragon," Freya said. "Who wasn't
going to give it up without a fight!"

Grunt plodded out on to the stage. One
of his dragon wings had come unstuck

and was dragging across the floor. The shaggy dog looked at the audience, then he looked at Vulgar and let out a puzzled woof.

"Back, foul creature!" Vulgar said, pointing his wooden sword at Grunt. "Or taste the blade of my sword."

Grunt opened his mouth and clamped his teeth over the end of the sword. His tail wagged happily.

"No, it's not a stick," Vulgar said. "Let go."

Vulgar tried to pull the sword away, but Grunt was having too much fun.

They pulled back and forth, playing tug-o'-war across the stage. Finally, Vulgar's grip slipped and he landed with a bump on his bum.

Grunt let out a bark of victory, then lay down and began chewing the sword. Vulgar glanced nervously at the audience, who were all guffawing loudly.

"Well, with the dragon out of the way, I can still get the treasure!" he cried, and he flung open the lid of the chest, revealing a stack of Helga's rolls. "Mine! The treasure is all mine!"

But Grunt had other ideas. He dropped the half-chewed sword and got stuck into the bread rolls. Vulgar watched in horror as his lumps of "gold" were wolfed down one by one.

Freya hopped to her feet and vanished behind the curtain. She emerged a moment later holding the golden helmet, then lay on her back and closed her eyes, the helmet clutched to her stomach.

"To claim the golden helmet, Sven had just one more task. He had to wake the sleeping princess with a kiss," she said.

"What?!" spluttered Vulgar. "No he didn't!"

"Yes he did," insisted Freya. "He kissed the princess."

Vulgar yanked the helmet from her hands and put it on his head. "No he didn't. Sven the Dragon-Slayer wouldn't kiss any stupid princess!"

Freya opened one eye and raised her head. "Yes. He. Did," she growled. "Now kiss the princess!"

The crowd chuckled. Vulgar shook his head. "No way! I'd rather kiss the dragon!"

The crowd giggled.

Freya jumped to her feet. "Kiss the princess!"

"No!"

"Then give me back the helmet!" Freya said, and she began to chase Vulgar around the stage.

"Get off! You're supposed to be asleep!"

"And *you're* supposed to give me a kiss!"

Freya cornered Vulgar at the front of the stage. She grabbed the golden helmet and they began to wrestle over it. The audience shrieked with laughter as they tussled and fought.

Having finished eating all the "gold", Grunt decided to get in on the act. He bounded across the stage, yelping and barking with excitement. Knut came running on to try to break up the fight, but his feet tangled in the curtain. There was a loud *rrrrrrip* and the curtain fell on top of him.

"Let go!" Freya snarled.

"You let go!" Vulgar hissed, and he heaved with all his might.

He yanked the helmet away from Freya, but he couldn't hold on to it. It spun over his shoulder. There was a loud thonk as the helmet flew off the stage and hit King Olaf on the top of the head.

The audience stopped laughing.

Freya and Vulgar stopped fighting.

Even Grunt stopped barking as King Olaf rubbed his head and slowly got to his feet. He glared at the children.

"Now you've done it," Harrumf muttered.

King Olaf raised both hands… and began to clap. "Bravo!" he said. "That was the funniest thing I've seen since Harrumf fell down the castle stairs."

A great cheer went up from the audience. Vulgar turned to see everyone clapping wildly. He glanced at Freya, and they both shrugged. The audience was still clapping when they returned to their seats, dragging the curtain – and Knut – behind them.

Helga leaned over a few rows of people and patted Vulgar on the shoulder. "Who knew we had such a little comedian on our hands?" she said, smiling.

Vulgar sighed. "It wasn't supposed to be funny. It was supposed to be scary," he mumbled, but no one heard him over the thunder of applause.

The clapping only died down when King Olaf took to the stage. "What a night it has been!" he boomed. "We've had laughs…"

Magnus the Magnificent stood up. "Thank you, Your Majesty."

"I wasn't talking about you," said King Olaf, and Magnus quickly sat down again. "We've had music, and we've had so much more. We have chosen a winner, but before I announce who it is, let's hear a big round of applause for our second-place competitors. Put your hands together for…"

The audience held its breath. Who would it be?

"The Dancing H's. Harald and Helga!"

Vulgar's parents stood up to a chorus of cheers. "Way to go, Mum and Dad!" Vulgar cried, as they took to the stage to accept their prize. It was a small trophy carved from stone and wood. They held it up and the crowd went wild.

"And now for the winner," said King Olaf, when Harald and Helga had left the stage. A hush fell over the audience. Vulgar felt Freya's hand grip his and he didn't even pull away.

King Olaf cleared his throat. "The winner of the Blubber Talent Contest is…"

He paused and looked out over the audience.

Vulgar waited.

The audience waited.

King Olaf took a deep breath and

roared, "The Bards of Blubber!"

The cheer almost lifted the roof off the Great Hall. Vulgar, Knut and Freya jumped up and raced on to the stage.

"A special trophy is in order, I think," said King Olaf. He picked up the golden helmet and put it on Vulgar's head. "Sven got his golden helmet in the end."

Freya leaned in and pecked Vulgar on the cheek. "And the princess got her kiss!"

The audience stamped their feet with delight. Vulgar grinned and took a deep bow. Maybe being funny was better than being scary, after all.